U0025477

Let's Enjoy Masterpieces!

GRADE 1

Beauty and the Beast

美女與野獸

Original Author Beaumont, Madame de
Adaptors David Desmond O'Flaherty
Illustrator Valentina Andreeva

WORDS 350

Let's Enjoy Masterpieces!

All the beautiful fairy tales and masterpieces that you have encountered during your childhood remain as warm memories in your adulthood. This time, let's indulge in the world of masterpieces through English. You can enjoy the depth and beauty of original works, which you can't enjoy through Chinese translations.

The stories are easy for you to understand because of your familiarity with them. When you enjoy reading, your ability to understand English will also rapidly improve.

This series of ***Let's Enjoy Masterpieces*** is a special reading comprehension booster program, devised to improve reading comprehension for beginners whose command of English is not satisfactory, or who are elementary, middle, and high school students. With this program, you can enjoy reading masterpieces in English with fun and efficiency.

This carefully planned program is composed of 5 levels, from the beginner level of 350 words to the intermediate and advanced levels of 1,000 words. With this program's level-by-level system, you are able to read famous texts in English and to savor the true pleasure of the world's language.

The program is well conceived, composed of reader-friendly explanations of English expressions and grammar, quizzes to help the student learn vocabulary and understand the meaning of the texts, and fabulous illustrations that adorn every page. In addition, with our "Guide to Listening," not only is reading comprehension enhanced but also listening comprehension skills are highlighted.

In the audio recording of the book, texts are vividly read by professional American voice actors. The texts are rewritten, according to the levels of the readers by an expert editorial staff of native speakers, on the basis of standard American English with the ministry of education recommended vocabulary. Therefore, it will be of great help even for all the students that want to learn English.

Please indulge yourself in the fun of reading and listening to English through ***Let's Enjoy Masterpieces***.

波茫特夫人

Beaumont,
Madame de
(1711–1780)

Madame Beaumont was a French writer. Right after her marriage, she moved to England. While she was working as a governess in England, she began to write an educational series of articles for newspapers in London, mainly based on stories drawn from folk tales, history, legends, and geography.

After she turned 40 years old, she began to publish her stories in many magazines. *Beauty and the Beast* was published in a magazine for children. In France, Beaumont was the first creator of a magazine for children, and she wrote stories and fairy tales in tune with the literary trend of liberal fantasy. She became one of the leading writers of romanticism.

Beauty and the Beast is a story about a beautiful girl and a beast.

Once upon a time, there was a rich merchant who had three daughters. Among his three daughters, the youngest was the most beautiful and kind.

One day the merchant lost his fortunes as his ships filled with all his fortunes were wrecked. Full of hope that one of his ships, long supposed to be lost, had arrived in a port with his fortune, he set off on a trip to the port. However, he went all the way to the port just to find out that his last ship was captured by pirates.

On the way back home, the poor merchant took shelter in the castle of a beast. As the merchant plucked a rose as a gift for his youngest daughter, he enraged the beast.

Finally, he came back home unharmed after he had promised to send his beautiful youngest daughter to the beast. In order to keep the promise, the beauty went to the castle of the beast and began to fall in love with the beast for his inner beauty and kind heart rather than his external ugliness.

Beauty and the Beast is a fairy tale, loved by readers of all ages. The story was also made into a Disney animated film.

How to Use This Book

本書使用說明

Chapter Four Don't Leave Me.

Chapter Four

Don't Leave Me.

A week later, the Beast returned[1] to the dining room. He looked embarrassed[2] and sad. "Beauty," he said. "I know that I'm a beast. And I know that a beauty could never marry a beast. Please, I'll just ask one thing of you. I want you to stay with me here forever[3]. Let's be friends. If you leave me, I'll be so lonely[4]. I think I would die of[5] sadness[6]."

Beauty looked at the ground and blushed[7]. "I'm sorry, Beast," she said. "I must go back[8] to my father. I saw him in the magical[9] mirror yesterday. He is living alone. My sisters finally[10] got married[11] and left him. He needs someone to take care of[12] him."

1 return [rɪˋtɝn] (v.) 返回
2 embarrassed [ɪmˋbærəst] (a.) 困窘的
3 forever [fəˋɛvɚ] (adv.) 永遠地
4 lonely [ˋlonlɪ] (a.) 寂寞的
5 die of 因……而死
6 sadness [ˋsædnɪs] (n.) 哀傷
7 blush [blʌʃ] (v.) 臉紅
8 go back 回去
9 magical [ˋmædʒɪkl] (a.) 魔法的
10 finally [ˋfaɪnlɪ] (adv.) 最後
11 get married 結婚
12 take care of 照顧

One Point Lesson
I'll ask one thing of you. 我有一件事情要請求你。
ask A of B：向B要求A
I asked nothing of you. 我沒對你要求任何東西。

58 Beauty and the Beast 59

1 *Original English texts*

It is easy to understand the meaning of the text, because the text is rewritten according to the levels of the readers.

2 *Explanation of the vocabulary*

The words and expressions that include vocabulary above the elementary level are clearly defined.

3 *Response notes*

Spaces are included in the book so you can take notes about what you don't understand or what you want to remember.

4 *One point lesson*

In-depth analyses of major grammar points and expressions help you to understand sentences with difficult grammar.

Audio Recording

In the audio recording, native speakers narrate the texts in standard American English. By combining the written words and the audio recording, you can listen to English with great ease.

Audio books have been popular in Britain and America for many decades. They allow the listener to experience the proper word pronunciation and sentence intonation that add important meaning and drama to spoken English. Students will benefit from listening to the recording twenty or more times.

After you are familiar with the text and recording, listen once more with your eyes closed to check your listening comprehension. Finally, after you can listen with your eyes closed and understand every word and every sentence, you are then ready to mimic the native speaker.

Then you should make a recording by reading the text yourself. Then play both recordings to compare your oral skills with those of a native speaker.

How to Improve Reading Ability

如何增進英文閱讀能力

1 *Catch key words*

Read the key words in the sentences and practice catching the gist of the meaning of the sentence. You might question how working with a few important words could enhance your reading ability. However, it's quite effective. If you continue to use this method, you will find out that the key words and your knowledge of people and situations enables you to understand the sentence.

2 *Divide long sentences*

Read in chunks of meaning, dividing sentences into meaningful chunks of information. In the book, chunks are arranged in sentences according to meaning. If you consider the sentences backwards or grammatically, your reading speed will be slow and you will find it difficult to listen to English.

You are ready to move to a more sophisticated level of comprehension when you find that narrowly focusing on chunks is irritating. Instead of considering the chunks, you will make it a habit to read the sentence from the beginning to the end to figure out the meaning of the whole.

3 *Make inferences and assumptions*

Making inferences and assumptions is part of your ability. If you don't know, try to guess the meaning of the words. Although you don't know all the words in context, don't go straight to the dictionary. Developing an ability to make inferences in the context is important.

The first way to figure out the meaning of a word is from its context. If you cannot make head or tail out of the meaning of a word, look at what comes before or after it. Ask yourself what can happen in such a situation. Make your best guess as to the word's meaning. Then check the explanations of the word in the book or look up the word in a dictionary.

4 *Read a lot and reread the same book many times*

There is no shortcut to mastering English. Only if you do a lot of reading will you make your way to the summit. Read fun and easy books with an average of less than one new word per page. Try to immerse yourself in English as often as you can.

Spend time "swimming" in English. Language learning research has shown that immersing yourself in English will help you improve your English, even though you may not be aware of what you're learning.

CONTENTS

Before you read
sunrise
日出
early in the morning
清早
leave home
離開家
go to the port
去港口
It took more than a week.
花了一個多星期的時間。
a small country-house
一間鄉下的小房子
arrive
到達
gold
黃金
You stole my rose!
你偷了我的玫瑰花！
angry
生氣
go back home
回家
growl
咆哮
Please, forgive me.
請原諒我！
kneel down
跪下
Thank you!
謝謝！
go to sleep
睡覺
grateful 感激
sit down
坐下
bed
床
eat
吃
candle
蠟燭
after supper
晚餐後
roasted chicken 烤雞
hot coffee
熱咖啡
delicious food 美味的食物
cake
蛋糕
have supper 吃晚餐

terrible news
可怕的消息
pirate
海盜
rain 雨
port
港
rob
搶劫
snow 雪
sad and cold
又難過又冷
miserable
悲慘的
sleep in the cold
睡在冷天中
a garden in front of the castle
城堡前的花園
sunset
日落
pick
摘
castle
城堡
wall
牆
rose bush
玫瑰花叢
gate
大門
warm 溫暖的
fireplace 壁爐
window 窗戶
look through
透過……看

Chapter One

1 Bring Me a Rose

Once[1], there was a rich merchant[2] in a big town. He had many ships. They brought[3] lots of gold from all over the world[4].

He also had three daughters. The two elder[5] sisters thought that they were the prettiest[6]. They would[7] only wear[8] expensive dresses. They would only think about marrying[9] rich men.

1 **once** [wʌns] (adv.) 曾經；以前
2 **merchant** [ˋmɝtʃənt] (n.) 商人
3 **bring** [brɪŋ] (v.) 帶來 (bring-brought-brought)
4 **all over the world** 全世界
5 **elder** [ˋɛldɚ] (a.) 年長的
6 **prettiest** 最漂亮的 (pretty 的最高級)
7 **would** [wʊd] (aux.)（過去）有……的習慣
8 **wear** [wɛr] (v.) 穿 (wear-wore-worn)
9 **marry** [ˋmærɪ] (v.) 結婚
10 **youngest** 最年輕的 (young 的最高級)
11 **in fact** 事實上
12 **beauty** [ˋbjutɪ] (n.) 美麗

The youngest[10] daughter was different.
She was the most beautiful daughter.
In fact[11], everything about her was beautiful.
This is why her name was "Beauty[12]."

One Point Lesson

This is why her name was "Beauty."
這也是她的名字叫做「美麗」的原因。

This is why . . . :「就這是為什麼……的原因了」

e.g. This is why I said "no." 這就是我說「不」的原因。

2

One day[1], the rich merchant suddenly[2] lost[3] everything. All of his ships sank[4]. Now he only had a small country-house[5].

The old merchant told his daughters what happened[6].

Beauty said to her father, "Please don't cry[7]. We have each other[8] and our good health[9]. Money is not important[10]."

1 **one day** 有一天
2 **suddenly** [ˋsʌdn̩lɪ] (adv.) 突然
3 **lose** [luz] (v.) 失去；損失 (lose-lost-lost)
4 **sink** [sɪŋk] (v.) 下沈；沈沒 (sink-sank-sunk)
5 **country-house** 鄉間住宅
6 **happen** [ˋhæpən] (v.) （偶然）發生
7 **cry** [kraɪ] (v.) 哭泣
8 **each other** 彼此
9 **health** [hɛlθ] (n.) 健康
10 **important** [ɪmˋpɔrtn̩t] (a.) 重要的

Her sisters started to pull their hair out[11].
"Oh, father," the eldest[12] daughter cried.
"What will we do now?"

"You'll have to work," he said, very sadly[13].

The middle[14] daughter was angry and said,
"We can't work. No rich man will want to[15]
marry us!"

11 **pull out** 拉長；拉著
12 **eldest** 最年長的（old 的最高級）
13 **sadly** [ˋsædlɪ] (adv.) 傷心地
14 **middle** [ˋmɪdl̩] (a.) 中間的
15 **want to** 想要

"Let's[1] go to town," said the eldest daughter. "We'll marry the first man that proposes[2]."

The two eldest daughters put on[3] their best dresses. They went to town, and looked for[4] husbands[5]. But everyone knew about the merchant's bad luck[6].

The middle daughter said to one man, "I'm ready to[7] be married[8]."

"I only wanted to marry you for your money!" said he.

1 **let's** 讓我們……
2 **propose** [prə`poz] (v.) 求婚
3 **put on** 穿上
4 **look for** 尋找
5 **husband** [`hʌzbənd] (n.) 丈夫
6 **bad luck** 不幸
7 **be ready to** 準備好
8 **be married** 結婚的；已婚的

Another man said to the eldest daughter, "I changed[9] my mind[10] because you don't have any money."

But one man ran to Beauty and said, "Please marry me. We could live happily[11] together."

But she couldn't leave[12] her father. "My father is old. I have to stay with[13] him."

9 **change** [tʃendʒ] (v.) 改變
10 **mind** [maɪnd] (n.) 意見
11 **happily** [ˋhæpɪlɪ] (adv.) 快樂地
12 **leave** [liv] (v.) 離開 (leave-left-left)
13 **stay with** 逗留；留下

4

The family moved to[1] the country-house.
The elder sisters didn't stop[2] complaining[3].
They never did any[4] work[5].

But Beauty worked hard[6] every day.
"If I don't work, my father will be hungry[7],"
she thought.

1 **move to** 搬到
2 **stop + V-ing** [stɑp] (v.) 停止做……
3 **complain** [kəmˋplen] (v.) 抱怨
4 **any** [ˋɛnɪ] (a.) 任何的
5 **work** [wɝk] (n.) 工作
6 **hard** [hɑrd] (adv.) 勞苦地
7 **hungry** [ˋhʌŋgrɪ] (a.) 飢餓的
8 **bring back** 帶回
9 **great** [gret] (a.) 極好的
10 **glad** [glæd] (a.) 高興的
11 **jump up** 跳起來
12 **for joy** 喜悅地
13 **shout** [ʃaut] (v.) 叫喊

One day, her father came home with a big smile. "I just heard some good news," he said. "One of my ships didn't sink. It's bringing back[8] lots of gold for us. We'll be rich again!"

Beauty smiled at her father. "That's great[9] news. I'm so glad[10] to see you happy again."

The two elder sisters jumped up[11] for joy[12]. "We're rich! We're rich!" they shouted[13].

One Point Lesson

If I **don't** work, my father **will** be hungry.
如果我不工作，我父親會挨餓。

If + 主詞 + 動詞現在式，主詞 + will + 動詞現在式：
假設語氣，表示「如果……，將會……」

e.g. **If** you **go** with me tomorrow, I'**ll** bring more food.
如果你明天和我一起去，我會帶更多食物回來。

5

The next morning, Beauty's father woke up[1] early[2]. He had to meet[3] his ship at the port[4]. "Good-bye, girls. I'm going to the port," he said.

The elder sisters jumped out of[5] bed and ran to him. "We had to eat bad food, and wear ugly[6] clothes," they said.

1 **wake up** 起床；醒來
2 **early** [ˋɝlɪ] (adv.) 早
3 **meet** [mit] (v.) 會面；遇見 (meet-met-met)
4 **port** [port] (n.) 港口
5 **out of** 向外；在外
6 **ugly** [ˋʌglɪ] (a.) 醜陋的
7 **present** [ˋprɛzn̩t] (n.) 禮物
8 **silk** [sɪlk] (n.) 絲
9 **bring back** 帶回
10 **What about you?** 那你呢？
11 **anything** [ˋɛnɪˏθɪŋ] (n.) 任何事物
12 **think of** 想到 (think-thought-thought)
13 **simple** [ˋsɪmp!] (a.) 簡單的
14 **just** [dʒʌst] (adv.) 僅；只要

"Will you bring us a present[7]? We want some chocolates and some silk[8] dresses."

"OK. I'll bring you back[9] what you want," he said. "What about you[10], Beauty? What can I get for you?"

Beauty didn't want anything[11]. She was happy just because she could see her father happy. She only thought[12] of one simple[13] thing.

"Just[14] bring me a rose," she said.

One Point Lesson

- **I'm going to** the port. 我要去港口。

be going to 將要；預定好要做

e.g. She's **going to** travel around the world.
她將會環遊全世界。

One Point Lesson

- It **took** him more than a week.
  這花了他一個多星期的時間。
- They have **taken** everything.
  他們把所有的東西都拿走了。

take：(1) 用於「花了……時間」，主詞通常用 it
(2) 拿走

e.g. **How long does it take to** go to the station?
到車站需要多少時間？

Then[1], the merchant said good-bye to them and left. The old man walked to the port. It took him more than[2] a week. When he got there, he heard some terrible[3] news.

His last[4] ship had no money on it. Pirates[5] robbed[6] it. They had taken everything[7].

Beauty's father fell[8] to the ground[9] and started to cry. "I must be[10] cursed[11]," he thought. Sadly he started to walk back home.

1 **then** [ðɛn] (adv.) 然後
2 **more than** 超過
3 **terrible** [ˋtɛrəbl̩] (a.) 恐怖的
4 **last** [læst] (a.) 最後的
5 **pirate** [ˋpaɪrət] (n.) 海盜
6 **rob** [rɑb] (v.) 搶劫
7 **everything** [ˋɛvrɪ͵θɪŋ] (n.) 一切
8 **fall to** 倒下；摔倒 (fall-fell-fallen)
9 **ground** [graʊnd] (n.) 地面
10 **must be** 一定是
11 **curse** [kɝs] (v.) 詛咒

A Circle the words related to "Beauty."

beautiful

lazy

greedy

nice

rose

money

B True or False.

T F ❶ He (Beauty's father) once had many ships.

T F ❷ He never had any money.

T F ❸ He loved his daughters.

T F ❹ He wasn't very old.

C Rewrite the sentences in future tense.

He *had* a ship. ⇨ He *will have* a ship.

1. They *brought* lots of gold for the merchant.

   ⇨ They ______________ lots of gold for the merchant.

2. Her sisters *started* to pull their hair out.

   ⇨ Her sisters ______________ to pull their hair out.

3. What *did* you do?

   ⇨ What ______________ you do?

D Rearrange the following sentences in chronological order.

1. Beauty asked her father to bring her a rose.
2. All of his ships sank.
3. The elder sisters looked for husband.
4. A rich merchant had many ships.
5. The family moved to the country-house.

______ ⇨ ______ ⇨ ______ ⇨ ______ ⇨ ______

7 Why Did You Steal[1] My Rose?

When the old man walked home, the weather became terribly[2] cold. The old man was sad and very cold. He thought it would be so miserable[3] to sleep in the cold[4].

1 **steal** [stil] (v.) 偷竊 (steal-stole-stolen)
2 **terribly** [ˋtɛrəbl̩ɪ] (adv.) 甚為
3 **miserable** [ˋmɪzərəbl̩] (a.) 悲慘的
4 **the cold** 嚴寒
5 **set** [sɛt] (v.)（太陽）下沈 (set-set-set)
6 **castle** [ˋkæsl̩] (n.) 城堡
7 **maybe** [ˋmebɪ] (adv.) 也許
8 **gate** [get] (n.) 大門
9 **yell** [jɛl] (v.) 呼喊
10 **look through** 透過⋯⋯看
11 **fireplace** [ˋfaɪr͵ples] (n.) 壁爐
12 **next to** 在⋯⋯旁邊
13 **roast** [rost] (v.) 烘烤
14 **lie down** 躺下
15 **comfortable** [ˋkʌmfɚtəbl̩] (a.) 舒服的
16 **go to sleep** 睡著

As the sun was setting[5], the merchant saw a castle[6]. "Maybe[7] there's a nice prince in that castle. He'll give me a bed tonight," he said.

When he came to the gates[8] of the castle, he yelled[9] "Hello!" Nobody answered him.

He looked through[10] a window and saw a fire in the fireplace[11]. Next to[12] the fireplace was a table. On the table were a roasted[13] chicken with potatoes, cake, and hot coffee. The food looked so delicious, and the castle looked so warm.

He walked in, sat down, and ate all of the food. After supper, he lay down[14] on a comfortable[15] bed and went to sleep[16].

8

When the old man woke up in the morning, he felt[1] very good. He saw the table was set with[2] a big breakfast. The old merchant felt grateful[3] to the owner[4] of the castle. He didn't know who he was. But he was saved[5] from[6] a cold and hungry night.

1 **feel** [fil] (v.) 感到；覺得 (feel-felt-felt)
2 **be set with** 以……準備 (set-set-set)
3 **grateful** [ˋgretfəl] (a.) 感激的
4 **owner** [ˋonɚ] (n.) 所有者
5 **save** [sev] (v.) 解救
6 **save A from B** 從 B 解救 A
7 **decide to** 決定要
8 **empty** [ˋɛmptɪ] (a.) 空的
9 **whoever** [huˋɛvɚ] (pron.) 無論是誰

The old man decided to[7] go and thank the owner. He walked all around the house. He saw a lot of beautiful furniture and big rooms, but he didn't see anybody. So he thanked the empty[8] castle.

"Thank you!" he yelled. "Whoever[9] you are!"

One Point Lesson

- He **felt** so good. 他心情非常好。

feel + 補語：「感到……」

e.g. I **felt** comfortable on the chair.
坐在椅子上我感覺很舒服。

e.g. He **looks** sick.
他看起來像生病了。

When he left, the old man saw a garden[1]. There were some rose bushes[2]. He remembered[3] Beauty's request[4]. As soon as[5] the old man picked[6] a rose, he heard a loud[7] growl[8]. The merchant jumped up[9], and saw a beast[10] running toward[11] him.

"You dirty, little thief[12]!" the Beast growled. "I gave you food and a bed. And what do you do? You steal my roses! Now you're going to pay for[13] it. I'm going to kill you!"

1 **garden** [ˋgɑrdn̩] (n.) 花園
2 **bush** [bʊʃ] (n.) 灌木叢
3 **remember** [rɪˋmɛmbɚ] (v.) 記得
4 **request** [rɪˋkwɛst] (n.) 要求
5 **as soon as** 一……就……
6 **pick** [pɪk] (v.) 摘；採
7 **loud** [laʊd] (a.) 大聲的
8 **growl** [graʊl] (v.) 咆哮
9 **jump up** 跳起來
10 **beast** [bist] (n.) 野獸
11 **toward** [təˋwɔrd] (prep.) 向
12 **thief** [θif] (n.) 小偷
13 **pay for** 付出代價 (pay-paid-paid)
14 **thump** [θʌmp] (v.) 怦怦地跳
15 **beat** [bit] (v.) 跳 (beat-beat-beat)
16 **my Lord** 大人

Thump-thump[14]! The old man's heart was beating[15] loudly. "Please, my Lord[16]. Please forgive[17] me. I didn't mean[18] to offend[19] you. I just wanted a rose for my youngest daughter," said he.

"I don't care about[20] that! And don't call[21] me 'my Lord.' My name is 'Beast.' That's what I am."

17 **forgive** [fɚˋgɪv] (v.) 原諒 (forgive-forgave-forgiven)
18 **mean** [min] (v.) 有意
19 **offend** [əˋfɛnd] (v.) 冒犯
20 **care about** 關心；在乎
21 **call** [kɔl] (v.) 稱呼

One Point Lesson

As soon as the old man picked the rose, he heard a loud growl. 老人一摘下玫瑰花，就聽到一聲響亮的怒吼。

as soon as + 主詞 + 動詞，主詞 + 動詞：一……就……

e.g. **As soon as** I bought this book, I sat down and read it.
我一買下這本書，就坐下讀了起來。

10

Then the Beast began to[1] think. "You say you have a daughter, eh[2]? You may[3] go home. But you have to send me your daughter. If your daughter doesn't come here, I'll kill you and your whole[4] family!"

The old man knew that the Beast wasn't joking[5], but the merchant didn't plan to[6] send his daughter.

"Beast," the old man said, "I have a problem[7]. I have no money to send her. Also, nobody else[8] in my family works. Without[9] her, the rest[10] of my family will starve[11]."

"Don't you worry[12] about that," said the Beast. "Take some gold from my castle. I have lots of it. Give the gold to your family."

1 **begin to** 開始做……
2 **eh** [e] (int.) 是嗎（表疑問或懷疑等）
3 **may** [me] (aux.) 可以
4 **whole** [hol] (a.) 全部的
5 **joke** [dʒok] (v.) 開玩笑
6 **plan to** 打算；計畫
7 **problem** [ˋprɑbləm] (n.) 問題
8 **else** [ɛls] (adv.) 另外；還
9 **without** [wɪˋðaʊt] (prep.) 沒有
10 **rest** [rɛst] (n.) 剩餘
11 **starve** [stɑrv] (v.) 飢餓；餓死
12 **worry** [ˋwɝɪ] (v.) 擔心

The old man took a bag of gold with him and started walking home. When the old man arrived home, he was tired[1] and very sad.

The elder daughters looked at his face and sighed[2]. They knew that something was wrong[3].

"Let me[4] guess[5]. The last boat sank, and we're still[6] poor," said the eldest daughter.

"Don't worry about money. We have lots of that," said the merchant. He opened his bag, and gold fell out[7] all over[8] the floor[9]. The elder daughters started filling[10] their pockets.

Beauty looked at her father and said, "I'm worried about[11] you. You look so sad."

"Actually[12], I'm sad because of this present," said the old man.

He took out[13] the rose, and gave it to Beauty. Then he told his daughters the sad story about the Beast, the castle, and the rose.

1 **tired** [ˋtaɪrd] (a.) 疲倦的
2 **sigh** [saɪ] (v.) 嘆息
3 **wrong** [rɔŋ] (a.) 不對的
4 **Let me** 讓我⋯⋯
5 **guess** [gɛs] (v.) 猜測
6 **still** [stɪl] (adv.) 仍然
7 **fall out** 掉出來 (fall-fell-fallen)
8 **all over** 到處
9 **floor** [flor] (n.) 地板
10 **fill** [fɪl] (v.) 裝滿；填滿
11 **be worried about** 擔心
12 **actually** [ˋæktʃuəlɪ] (adv.) 實際上
13 **take out** 拿出來

One Point Lesson

I'm sad **because of** this present. 我因這份禮物而感到難過。

① **because + 主詞 + 動詞／because of + 名詞**：因為⋯⋯

e.g. I was happy **because** he gave me a rose.
我因為他送我玫瑰花而感到開心。

e.g. I'm sad **because of** him. 我因他而感到傷心。

The elder daughters didn't care[1] about his story. They were happy playing with[2] their gold. But Beauty couldn't stop[3] crying. "Oh, this is awful[4]. This is all my fault[5]."

After a while[6], Beauty said quietly, "I'm going to[7] go to the Beast, father."

Beauty's father looked at his daughter.

"There is no choice[8]," she said. "The beast will kill you and our whole family if[9] I don't go."

1 **care** [kɛr] (v.) 掛念；擔心
2 **play with** 把玩
3 **stop + V-ing** 停止做……
(stop-stopped-stopped)
4 **awful** [ˋɔfʊl] (a.) 可怕的
5 **fault** [fɔlt] (n.) 錯誤
6 **after a while** 過了一會兒
7 **be going to** 將要
8 **choice** [tʃɔɪs] (n.) 選擇
9 **if** [ɪf] (conj.) 如果
10 **determined** [dɪˋtɝmɪnd] (a.) 堅決的
11 **be no use + V-ing** 沒有用

She looked determined[10].
There was no use telling[11] her not to go.
Beauty always did what she said.

One Point Lesson

- I'm **going to** go to the Beast, father.
  我會去找野獸的，父親。

be going to： 即將……

e.g. I'm **going to** go to bed. 我要去睡了。
e.g. What **are** you **going to** do with it? 那你打算怎麼辦？

Comprehension Quiz Chapter Two

A Fill in the blanks with the given words.

1. The old man ____________ a rose in the garden.

2. The merchant ____________ a roasted chicken.

3. The old man ____________ through a window.

4. The old man ________ toward home.

B True or False.

T F ❶ Beauty's elder sisters liked to wear expensive clothing.

T F ❷ Beauty's elder sisters liked to eat any kind of food.

T F ❸ Beauty's elder sisters loved money.

C Match the two parts of each sentence.

❶ The weather	• •	Ⓐ was miserable.
❷ The Beast	• •	Ⓑ was beating very loudly.
❸ The old man's heart	• •	Ⓒ became terribly cold.
❹ The old man	• •	Ⓓ became very angry.

D Rearrange the following sentences in chronological order.

❶ The old man went to bed.

❷ The old man ate the entire breakfast.

❸ The weather became very cold.

❹ The old man picked a rose.

_____ ⇨ _____ ⇨ _____ ⇨ _____

Before you read
curtain 窗簾
thousands of books
上千本書
computer
電腦
grandfather clock
座鐘；老爺鐘
window
窗戶
bookshelf
書架
desk 書桌
armchair
扶手椅
library 書房
The clock is standing by the window.
時鐘立在窗戶旁邊。
kitchen 廚房
dining room 飯廳
kettle
水壺
pot
鍋
pan
煎鍋
sink
水槽
wall paper
壁紙
vase
花瓶
table
餐桌
dish
盤子
refrigerator
冰箱
chair
椅子
spoon 湯匙
fork 叉子
grill
烤架
dish washer
洗碗機
bottle
瓶子
knife
刀
napkin
餐巾
The dining room is next to the kitchen.
飯廳就在廚房隔壁。
hall 廳廊
He saw a lot of beautiful furniture and big rooms.
他看到很多華麗的家具和大房間。
carpet
地毯

bathroom 浴室
bedroom 臥室
toothbrush 牙刷
shampoo 洗髮精
toothpaste 牙膏
mirror 鏡子
wardrobe 衣櫥
lamp 檯燈
chandelier 吊燈
pillow 枕頭
washstand 盥洗臺
bathtub 浴缸
chest of drawers 五斗櫃
bed 床
soap 香皂
toilet 馬桶
towel 毛巾
There's a pillow lying on the bed.
床上擺著一個枕頭。
second floor 二樓
living room 客廳
upstairs 樓上
painting 繪畫
paintings on the wall 掛在牆上的畫
television 電視
fireplace 壁爐
piano 鋼琴
stairs 樓梯
stool 凳子
sofa 沙發
floor 地板
downstairs 樓下
furniture 家具
first floor 一樓
There were fine curtains and expensive carpets, but no people.
那裡有精美的窗簾、昂貴的地毯，但沒有人。
flower pot 花盆

The Beast Is Going to Eat Me

The next morning, Beauty left for[1] the castle. She asked people for directions[2]. The castle was very famous[3], because it was the biggest[4] one around. At sunset[5], she reached[6] it.

Beauty looked around[7] the castle. Like her father, she saw nobody. She yelled, "Hello!" but no one answered. She came in and saw a table with food on it. Beauty thought, "This beast must be trying to[8] make me fatter[9]. I think he's going to eat me." Beauty ate everything on the table.

After supper[10], she walked around the castle. There were the fine curtains and expensive carpets, but no people. She saw a library[11] with thousands of[12] books. But there were no people reading them. Then, Beauty came to a door. On it was a sign[13] that read[14] "BEAUTY'S APARTMENT[15]."

1 **leave for** 動身去
2 **direction** [dəˋrɛktʃən] (n.) 方向
3 **famous** [ˋfeməs] (a.) 著名的
4 **biggest** 最大的 (big-bigger-biggest)
5 **sunset** [ˋsʌnˏsɛt] (n.) 落日
6 **reach** [ritʃ] (v.) 到達
7 **look around** 四下觀望
8 **try to** 試圖；努力
9 **fatter** 更胖的 (fat-fatter-fattest)
10 **supper** [ˋsʌpɚ] (n.) 晚餐
11 **library** [ˋlaɪˏbrɛrɪ] (n.) 圖書室
12 **thousands of** 數千的
13 **sign** [saɪn] (n.) 牌子
14 **read** [rid] (v.) 寫明 (read-read-read)
15 **apartment** [əˋpɑrtmənt] (n.) 房間

One Point Lesson

This beast must be trying to **make me fatter.**
這野獸一定是想要讓我變胖。

make + 受詞 + 補語（形容詞／分詞／不定詞原形）： 使……成為

e.g. The funny story **made her laugh.**
那有趣的故事讓她笑了出來。

14

"Is this my room? Maybe he won't[1] kill me. And how[2] does he know my name?" she thought.

Beauty opened the door and went inside[3]. The girl was amazed by[4] the room. It was filled with[5] beautiful things. The room was as beautiful as Beauty. The girl was so happy to be there.

She smiled and jumped on[6] the bed.
A golden[7] book was lying on[8] the bed.
The title was "BEAUTY'S BOOK."

She opened the book and read the first page. It read, "Welcome[9], Beauty. Don't worry about[10] anything. No one will hurt[11] you in this castle. You are the princess[12] here. If you want anything, just say so. Invisible[13] people will bring you what you want[14]."

1 **won't** 不會（will not 的縮寫）
2 **how** [hau] (adv.) 如何
3 **inside** [ɪnˋsaɪd] (prep.) 往裡面
4 **be amazed by** 因……吃驚
5 **be filled with** 用……填滿
6 **jump on** 跳到……上
7 **golden** [ˋgoldn̩] (a.) 金色的
8 **lie on** 躺在…… (lie-lay-lain)
9 **welcome** [ˋwɛlkəm] (int.) 歡迎
10 **don't worry about** 別擔心
11 **hurt** [hɝt] (v.) 使受傷；危害
12 **princess** [ˋprɪnsɪs] (n.) 公主
13 **invisible** [ɪnˋvɪzəbl̩] (a.) 看不見的
14 **what you want** 凡是你想要的事物

15

"I want to see my poor[1] father. He must be very sad." As soon as Beauty said this, a picture of her home appeared[2] in a mirror in front of[3] her.

She saw her father sitting in[4] his favorite[5] chair. He looked so sad. She also saw her two sisters playing with gold.

She thought, "He will learn[6] to live without me soon. He'll be happy again."

After a while, she fell asleep[7] thinking about her family.

1 **poor** [pʊr] (a.) 可憐的
2 **appear** [əˋpɪr] (v.) 出現
3 **in front of** 在……前面
4 **sit in** 坐在……
5 **favorite** [ˋfevərɪt] (a.) 特別喜愛的
6 **learn** [lɝn] (v.) 學習
7 **fall asleep** 睡著

One Point Lesson

She **saw her father sitting** in his favorite chair.
她看到父親坐在他最喜歡的椅子上。

see + sb. + V-ing：看到某人在什麼做……

e.g. I **saw him playing** tennis. 我那時看到他在打網球。

16

Beauty spent the next day alone[1]. In the evening, she sat down to a wonderful supper. When she picked up[2] her knife and fork, she heard a gentle[3] growl from behind[4] her.

"Beauty," said the Beast. "May I have supper with you?"

"It is your castle," Beauty answered. "You can do what you want."

"No," said the Beast. "You are the princess of this castle. You should decide. I don't want you to feel uncomfortable[5]."

"You seem to[6] be very gentle," she said.

The Beast raised[7] his ugly eyebrows[8]. He hadn't expected her to[9] say this.

"You speak so gently[10]," Beauty continued[11]. "You are probably[12] more handsome on the inside."

"Aw, I don't know about that. Thank you for saying so," said the Beast shyly[13]. "I will join[14] you for supper."

1 **alone** [əˋlon] (adv.) 獨自地
2 **pick up** 拿起
3 **gentle** [ˋdʒɛntḷ] (a.) 溫柔的
4 **behind** [bɪˋhaɪnd] (prep.) 在……後面
5 **uncomfortable** [ʌnˋkʌmfətəbḷ] (a.) 不舒服的
6 **seem to** 似乎；看來好像
7 **raise** [rez] (v.) 抬起
8 **eyebrow** [ˋaɪ͵braʊ] (n.) 眉毛
9 **expect to** 預期……發生
10 **gently** [ˋdʒɛntlɪ] (adv.) 溫柔地
11 **continue** [kənˋtɪnjʊ] (v.) 繼續
12 **probably** [ˋprɑbəblɪ] (adv.) 大概；或許
13 **shyly** [ˋʃaɪlɪ] (adv.) 羞怯地
14 **join** [dʒɔɪn] (v.) 加入

One Point Lesson

May I have supper with you? 我可以與你共進晚餐嗎？

May I . . . ? 我可以……嗎？（口氣較為客氣）
Can I . . . ? 我能……嗎？

e.g. May I borrow your book? 我可以借你的書嗎？
e.g. Can I use your pencil? 我能用你的鉛筆嗎？

17

That evening, Beauty and the Beast sat down, and ate together. They spent a long time talking. At the end[1] of the evening, Beauty thought that the Beast was not so scary[2].

Every evening, he would have supper with her. They talked about many things. But the Beast asked one thing every night.
"How ugly am I?"

1 **at the end of** 在……的最後
2 **scary** [ˋskɛrɪ] (a.) 令人害怕的
3 **that way** 那樣的情況
4 **at all** 根本；絲毫
5 **lie** [laɪ] (v.) 說謊 (lie-lied-lied)
6 **good-looking** (a.) 好看的

Beauty always said, "Your heart is beautiful." She really felt that way[3].

"I may be nice, but I am still a beast," he said.

A strange thing happened. Beauty began to think that the Beast wasn't ugly at all[4]. He seemed to become handsome to her.

The Beast knew that Beauty never lied[5]. He didn't believe that he was good-looking[6]. But he did believe that Beauty saw something handsome inside him.

One Point Lesson

- Beauty saw **something handsome** inside him. 美麗看見他內心美好的一面。

---

something（某事某物）、anything（任何東西）
→ 後面通常接形容詞作修飾。

e.g. Is there **anything wrong**? 有什麼不對嗎？
e.g. He knew **something important**.
他知道了些重要的事。

The Beast felt a love for Beauty the first time[1] that he saw her. The problem was that she couldn't love him. "It is difficult to love an ugly beast," he thought.

He often imagined[2] that they were married[3]. It wasn't very difficult. They slept under the same roof[4], and ate the same food.

Every evening they talked for hours[5] like a husband and wife. But there was one thing missing[6]: Beauty didn't love him.

Then, one day, he couldn't hide[7] his feelings[8].
"I love you, Beauty," he said. "Please marry[9] me."

She sat and looked at the Beast for a long time.
"You are kind and gentle," said Beauty.
"But you are a beast. And I can't imagine being married to a beast. I'm sorry."

The Beast growled and ran away[10]. He stayed[11] at his room for a week after that night. Beauty had to[12] eat dinner alone.

1 **the first time** 第一次
2 **imagine** [ɪ`mædʒɪn] (v.) 想像
3 **married** [`mærɪd] (a.) 已婚的
4 **under the same roof** 在同一個屋簷下
5 **for hours** 好幾個小時
6 **missing** [`mɪsɪŋ] (a.) 缺少的
7 **hide** [haɪd] **(v.)** 隱藏；隱瞞 (hide-hid-hidden)
8 **feeling** [`filɪŋ] (n.) 感覺；情緒
9 **marry** [`mærɪ] (v.) 結婚
10 **run away** 跑走
11 **stay** [ste] (v.) 停留；留下
12 **had to** 必須（have to 的過去式）

A Crosswords.

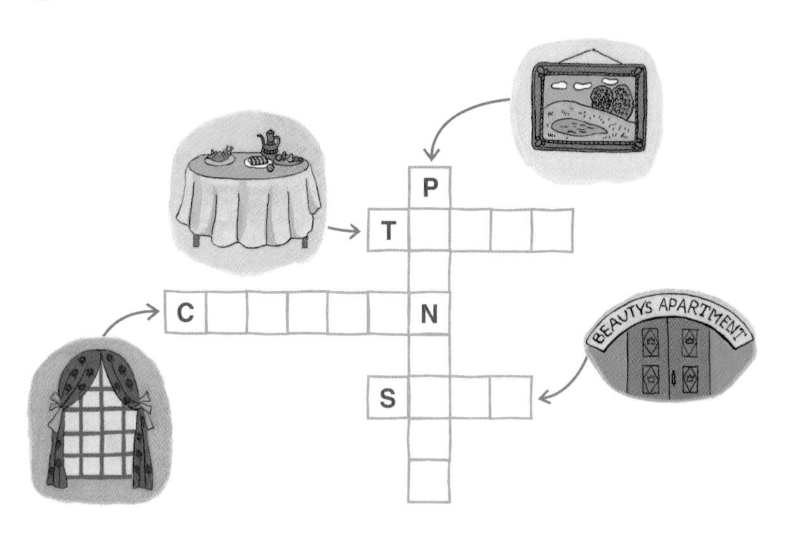

B Fill in the blanks with the given words.

believed imagined spent appeared

1. A picture of Beauty's house ______________ in a mirror.
2. He often ______________ that they were married.
3. They ______________ a long time talking.
4. He ______________ that Beauty saw something handsome inside him.

C Match the two parts of each sentence.

❶ The castle was well known •	• Ⓐ	with the gold.
❷ They were still playing •	• Ⓑ	but there were no people reading them.
❸ She saw many books •	• Ⓒ	who was sitting in his favorite chair.
❹ She saw her father •	• Ⓓ	because it was the biggest one around.

D Rearrange the following sentences in chronological order.

❶ Beauty came to a door on which has a sign "BEAUTY'S APARTMENT."

❷ The Beast asked Beauty if he could eat supper with her.

❸ The Beast asked Beauty to marry him.

❹ Beauty left for the castle.

_____ ⇨ _____ ⇨ _____ ⇨ _____

Don't Leave Me

A week later, the Beast returned[1] to the dining room. He looked embarrassed[2] and sad. "Beauty," he said. "I know that I'm a beast. And I know that a beauty could never marry a beast. Please, I'll just ask one thing of you. I want you to stay with me here forever[3]. Let's be friends. If you leave me, I'll be so lonely[4]. I think I would die of[5] sadness[6]."

Beauty looked at the ground and blushed[7].
"I'm sorry, Beast," she said. "I must go back[8] to my father. I saw him in the magical[9] mirror yesterday. He is living alone. My sisters finally[10] got married[11] and left him. He needs someone to take care of[12] him."

1 **return** [rɪ`tɝn] (v.) 返回
2 **embarrassed** [ɪm`bærəst] (a.) 困窘的
3 **forever** [fɚ`ɛvɚ] (adv.) 永遠地
4 **lonely** [`lonlɪ] (a.) 寂寞的
5 **die of** 因……而死
6 **sadness** [`sædnɪs] (n.) 哀傷
7 **blush** [blʌʃ] (v.) 臉紅
8 **go back** 回去
9 **magical** [`mædʒɪkl̩] (a.) 魔法的
10 **finally** [`faɪnl̩ɪ] (adv.) 最後
11 **get married** 結婚
12 **take care of** 照顧

One Point Lesson

I'll **ask** one thing **of** you.
我有一件事情要請求你。

ask A of B：向 B 要求 A

e.g. I **asked** nothing **of** you. 我沒對你要求任何東西。

20

"I understand[1] you, Beauty. You are so kind," said the beast. "I know that you have to be with[2] your father. But I can't stay alone anymore[3]. Go home for a week. I'll send lots of money to your house. Get a good servant[4] for your father. The servant could take care of him. Then, come back[5] to me. If you don't come back, I will die of heartbreak[6]," he said.

1 **understand** [ˏʌndɚˋstænd] (v.) 理解 (understand-understood-understood)
2 **be with** 與……一起
3 **anymore** [ˋɛnɪmɔr] (adv.) 再也（不）
4 **servant** [ˋsɝvənt] (n.) 僕人
5 **come back** 回來
6 **heartbreak** [ˋhɑrtˏbrek] (n.) 心碎

"Alright[7], Beast," said Beauty. "My father will be happy just[8] to see me again[9]."

"Take this ring[10]," the Beast said. "Wear[11] it. When you want to come back to me, take the ring off[12] before going to bed[13]. In the morning, you'll wake up here in my castle."

7 **alright** [ˋɔlˋraɪt] (adv.) 沒問題 (= all right)
8 **just** [dʒʌst] (adv.) 僅；只要
9 **again** [əˋgɛn] (adv.) 再度
10 **ring** [rɪŋ] (n.) 戒指
11 **wear** [wɛr] (v.) 戴 (wear-wore-worn)
12 **take off** 脫下；移去
13 **go to bed** 睡覺

21

Beauty put the ring on[1], and went to bed.

In the morning, she woke up in her father's house. She saw a box in the corner[2] of the room. It was full of[3] gold and beautiful dresses. The dresses were made of[4] jewels and silver.

Beauty knew that these were presents from the beast. "Thank you, Beast," she said to herself[5].

1 **put on** 穿上；戴上
2 **corner** [ˋkɔrnɚ] (n.) 角落
3 **be full of** 充滿著
4 **be made of** 用……做成
5 **to herself** 對她自己
6 **tear** [tɪr] **(n.)** 眼淚
7 **joy** [dʒɔɪ] **(n.)** 喜悅
8 **gift** [gɪft] **(n.)** 禮物
9 **heaven** [ˋhɛvən] (n.) 天堂
10 **hug** [hʌg] **(v.)** 擁抱

When the lonely old merchant saw Beauty, he began to cry. His tears[6] were tears of joy[7].

"You are a gift[8] from heaven[9]," he said. "I thought the Beast ate you."

The merchant hugged[10] his daughter for a long time. They were so happy.

One Point Lesson

- **Wear** it. 戴上它。
- **Take** the ring **off**. 拔下戒指。
- Beauty **put** the ring **on**. 美麗把戒指戴上。

---

put on/wear：穿戴（衣服、鞋子、戒指、配件等）
put on 是穿上衣服的動作，wear 則表示穿上的狀態。

Take off：脫掉（衣服、鞋子、戒指、配件等）

e.g. She is **wearing** a beautiful dress. 她身穿一件美麗的禮服。

e.g. The boy **put on** his school uniform quickly.
男孩匆忙把校服穿上。

A few[1] days later, her sisters came with their husbands. They were married to rich and handsome men, but they didn't look happy. This was because of their husbands.

When Beauty saw these men, she began to think a lot[2] about[3] the Beast. They were handsome, and he was ugly. They were boring[4], and the Beast was interesting.[5] They were mean[6], and the Beast was kind. They were stingy[7], and the Beast was generous[8].

They made their wives[9] feel sad,
but the Beast made Beauty feel happy.
As Beauty thought about the Beast, she smiled. Beauty realized[10] at that very[11] moment[12] that she loved the Beast.

The middle sister saw the smile, and became very angry. "She looks happy but I'm so sad. I can't stand[13] this!
I wish she were dead!"

1 **a few** 一些（後接可數名詞）
2 **a lot** 許多
3 **think about** 考慮；想
4 **boring** [ˋborɪŋ] (a.) 無聊的
5 **interesting** [ˋɪntərɪstɪŋ] (a.) 有趣的
6 **mean** [min] (a.) 壞心眼的
7 **stingy** [ˋstɪŋdʒɪ] (a.) 吝嗇的
8 **generous** [ˋdʒɛnərəs] (a.) 慷慨的
9 **wife** [waɪf] (n.) 妻子（複數：wives）
10 **realize** [ˋrɪəˏlaɪz] (v.) 明白
11 **very** [ˋvɛrɪ] (a.) 正是
12 **moment** [ˋmomənt] (n.) 瞬間
13 **stand** [stænd] (v.) 容忍 (stand-stood-stood)

One Point Lesson

They were married to rich and handsome men.
她們嫁給了有錢又英俊的男人。

---

married to：結婚的；與……結婚的
marry：與……結婚（marry 後面不加介系詞）

e.g. I got **married to** a good man. 我嫁給了一個好男人。
e.g. I will **marry** her when I grow up. 等我長大後要娶她。

"I have a plan[1]," said the middle sister to the eldest. "Let's keep[2] Beauty here longer than a week. Then[3], the Beast will become very angry. He'll eat Beauty when she goes back to the castle."

The eldest sister agreed. She was always jealous[4] because Beauty was more beautiful.

"Let's be really nice to her. Then she won't want to leave," said the eldest.

One Point Lesson

- Then, the Beast will **become** very **angry**.
  那樣野獸一定會很生氣。

---

become + 形容詞或名詞：變得……；成為……

e.g. **become tired** 變得疲累

e.g. He **became a scientist**. 他成為一位科學家。

For a few days, the elder sisters were very nice to Beauty. They brought[5] her gifts. They worked around their father's house. They said nice things to her.

"Poor Beauty," said the eldest. "You worked so hard. You should take a rest[6]."

1 **plan** [plæn] (n.) 計畫
2 **keep** [kip] (v.) 留住 (keep-kept-kept)
3 **then** [ðɛn] (conj.) 然後
4 **jealous** [ˋdʒɛləs] (a.) 嫉妒
5 **bring** [brɪŋ] (v.) 帶來 (bring-brought-brought)
6 **take a rest** 休息

24

On the sixth[1] day, Beauty went to town, and hired[2] a good servant. That evening, Beauty came back home with the woman. "I hired a good servant for you, father. She'll take good care of[3] you. I'll say good-bye to all of you now."

Then, the elder sisters started to cry. "Oh, you can't leave us," said the middle sister. "We're just[4] getting to[5] really know you. I want to talk to you some more."

"Please, please," said the eldest. "Stay for[6] one more week."

Beauty couldn't stand to see them sad. "Alright," she said. "I'll stay for just one more week[7]."

1 **sixth** [sɪksθ] (a.) 第六的
2 **hire** [haɪr] (v.) 雇用
3 **take (good)** care of（好好）照顧
4 **just** [dʒʌst] (adv.) 剛才
5 **get to** 開始……
6 **stay for** 停留……時間
7 **one more week** 再一星期

A Complete the sentences with antonyms of the adjectives underlined.

1. He was ______________________.
   handsome
2. He was ______________________.
   boring
3. He was ______________________.
   mean
4. He was ______________________.
   stingy
5. He made Beauty feel ______________________.
   sad

B True or False.

T F 1. Beauty woke up in her father's house.

T F 2. Beauty hired a good servant for her father.

T F 3. A week later, Beauty returned to the castle.

T F 4. Beauty liked her sisters' husbands.

T F 5. Beauty decided to stay home forever.

C Fill in the blanks with the given words.

servant smile left

1. My sisters finally got married, and __________ father.
2. The sisters saw her __________, and became very angry.
3. Get a good __________ to take care of your father.

D Match the two parts of each sentence.

1 He'll eat Beauty •		• A from heaven.
2 You are a gift •		• B but I'm so sad.
3 I want you to stay •		• C with me here forever.
4 If you leave me, •		• D when she goes back to the castle
5 She looks happy •		• E I'll be so lonely.

25 I Love You, Beast

A few evenings later, Beauty had a terrible[1] dream. In the dream, she walked around the castle, and looked for[2] the Beast. There was nobody there. She called his name, but she didn't hear an answer.

Nearby[3] the castle, she heard a noise[4]. When she walked toward[5] the noise, she found[6] the Beast.

He was lying on the ground. "Oh, Beast! Please don't die[7]," she cried[8].

"I am so ugly, aren't I?" he growled. "You could never love a beast like me." Then the Beast died in her arms[9].

Beauty woke up and jumped out of[10] bed. "What am I doing? I'm killing my poor Beast. I must go to the Beast right now[11] and marry him!"

Beauty wrote a good-bye letter[12] to her father. Then, she took off her ring, and fell asleep[13] again.

1 **terrible** [ˋtɛrəbḷ] (a.) 可怕的
2 **look for** 尋找
3 **nearby** [ˋnɪrˏbaɪ] (adv.) 附近
4 **noise** [nɔɪz] (n.) 聲響
5 **toward** [təˋwɔrd] (prep.) 朝向
6 **find** [faɪnd] (v.) 發現 (find-found-found)
7 **die** [daɪ] (v.) 死
8 **cry** [kraɪ] (v.) 叫喊 (cry-cried-cried)
9 **in one's arm** 在某人的臂彎裡
10 **out of** 自……離開
11 **right now** 就是現在
12 **good-bye letter** 道別信
13 **fall asleep** 睡著

In the morning, Beauty woke up in the castle. She walked around, and looked for the Beast. He was not anywhere. She thought that he would appear[1] at the dinner table as usual[2]. "Tonight[3], I'll tell him that I'll marry him." That evening, Beauty made herself beautiful[4].

1 **appear** [ə`pɪr] (v.) 出現
2 **as usual** 像平常一樣
3 **tonight** [tə`naɪt] (n.) 今晚
4 **make oneself beautiful** 讓自己看起來很美

At dinnertime[5], she didn't see any food magically[6] appear. The Beast didn't come to dinner, either.

Then Beauty thought, "Maybe he's dead. Maybe he died when I didn't come back to him. Maybe he couldn't live any longer[7], because I wouldn't marry him."

5 **dinnertime** [ˋdɪnɚˏtaɪm] (n.) 用餐時間

6 **magically** [ˋmædʒɪklɪ] (adv.) 如魔法般地

7 **any longer** 已經；再（用於否定句）

27

"Beast! Beast!" she called out[1]. But there was no answer.

Then she remembered the place where she found the Beast in her dream. She ran there very quickly. She found the Beast lying in the garden. Just like[2] in her dream, he seemed to be dying[3].

1 **call out** 呼喊
2 **just like** 就像；就如同
3 **dying** [ˋdaɪɪŋ] (a.) 垂死的
4 **bend over** 俯身 (bend-bent-bent)
5 **creature** [ˋkritʃɚ] (n.) 生物
6 **hold** [hold] (v.) 抓住
7 **hairy** [ˋhɛrɪ] (a.) 多毛的
8 **cheek** [tʃik] (n.) 臉頰
9 **bright** [braɪt] (a.) 明亮的
10 **flash** [flæʃ]] (n.) 閃光
11 **light** [laɪt] (n.) 光亮

"Beast!" she cried. "You can't die. You must live with me, and be my husband! Please, marry me."

Then Beauty bent over[4] the dying creature[5], and held[6] him in her arms. Then she kissed the hairy[7] Beast's cheek[8]. At that moment, she saw a bright[9] flash[10] of light[11] .

28

In a moment[1], Beauty found herself inside the castle. The room was filled with[2] flowers. Next to[3] Beauty was a very handsome man. He was dressed like[4] a prince. She was very confused[5]. "What's going on here? Where's my dear[6] Beast?"

"I am your Beast, sweet[7] Beauty," the prince said. "A long time ago, an evil[8] witch[9] cast a spell[10] on me. She changed me into[11] a beast. She said that I would never change or grow old[12] until[13] a beautiful woman agreed to marry me. I lived by myself[14] for hundreds of years. When you came to my place, I felt happy for the first time in centuries[15]. But when you said you wouldn't marry me, I felt like[16] I would die. Then you came back, and said you would marry me. You saved[17] my life. And you changed me back to my natural[18] form[19]. I owe[20] you everything, dear Beauty. And I love you very much."

1 **in a moment** 立即
2 **be filled with** 充滿……
3 **next to** 緊鄰的
4 **dressed like** 穿著似……
5 **confused** [kənˋfjuzd] (a.) 困惑的
6 **dear** [dɪr] (a.) 親愛的
7 **sweet** [swit] (a.) 可愛的
8 **evil** [ˋivḷ] (a.) 邪惡的

9 **witch** [wɪtʃ] (n.) 女巫
10 **cast a spell** 施魔咒
11 **change into** 變成……
12 **grow old** 變老
13 **until** [ənˋtɪl] (conj.) 直到
14 **myself** [maɪˋsɛlf] (pron.) 我自己
15 **in centuries** 好幾個世紀（單數：century）
16 **feel like** 感到好似
17 **save** [sev] (v.) 拯救
18 **natural** [ˋnætʃərəl] (a.) 天生的
19 **form** [fɔrm] (n.) 外型
20 **owe** [o] (v.) 欠人恩情

29

At that moment, a good witch appeared and said to them, "I'm glad to see you looking so handsome again, sir[1]. Beauty, you finally met a beautiful person like you. Truly, you are the most handsome couple[2] in the whole world. I will marry you today. And I will give you happiness[3] for the rest of your lives[4]. I will bring you many happy and beautiful children, too."

1 **sir** [sɝ] (n.) 先生；閣下
2 **couple** [ˋkʌpl̩] (n.) 夫婦；一對
3 **happiness** [ˋhæpɪnɪs] (n.) 幸福；快樂
4 **lives** [laɪvz] (n.) 生命（life 的複數）
5 **be born** 出生 (bear-bore-born)
6 **laughter** [ˋlæftɚ] (n.) 笑聲

From that day, Beauty and her prince were always happy. They continued having their long talks in the evenings.

And when their children were born[5], the halls of the castle were filled with children's laughter[6].

Comprehension Quiz Chapter Five

A Fill in the blanks with the given words.

crying happy dressed wrote

❶ ❷ ❸ ❹

❶ Beauty __________ a good-bye letter to her father.

❷ They were __________ and laughed often.

❸ She started __________.

❹ He was __________ like a prince.

B True or False.

T F ❶ A good witch turned Beauty into Beast.

T F ❷ Beauty had a terrible dream.

T F ❸ The Beast was happy in the Beauty's dream.

T F ❹ An evil witch cast a spell on the Beast.

C Rewrite the sentences in negative form.

She heard some answer.

⇨ She didn't hear any answer.

1. At dinnertime, she saw some food magically appear.

   ⇨ At dinnertime, she ____________ food magically appear.

2. An evil witch cast a spell on me.

   ⇨ An evil witch ____________ a spell on me.

3. You were the most handsome couple.

   ⇨ You ____________ the most handsome couple.

D Rearrange the following sentences in chronological order.

1. Beauty and the Beast got married.
2. Beauty stood beside a handsome prince.
3. Beauty woke up in the castle.
4. Beauty had a bad dream.
5. Beauty found the Beast in the garden, just like in the dream.

_____ ⇨ _____ ⇨ _____ ⇨ _____ ⇨ _____

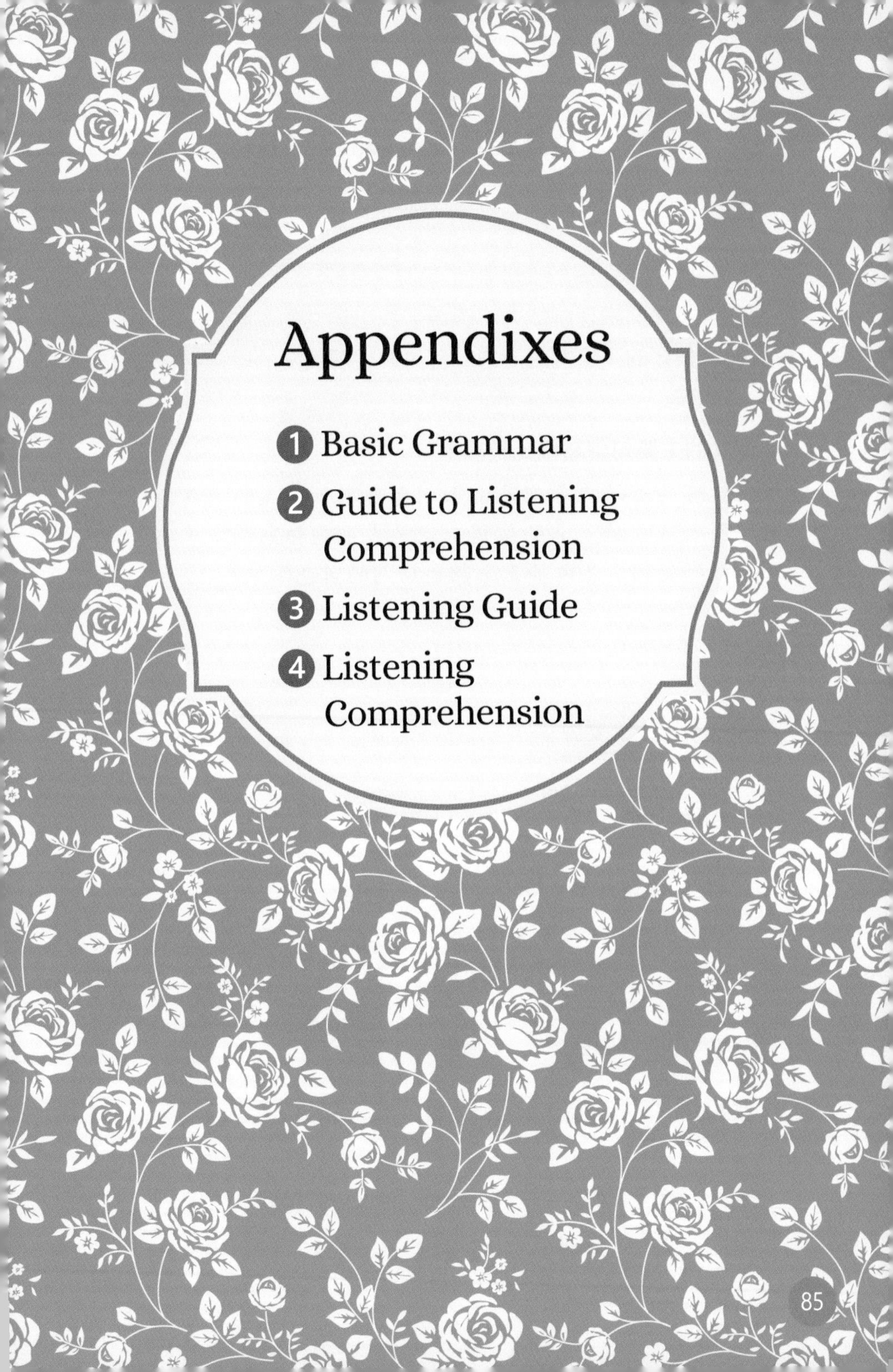

Appendixes

1. Basic Grammar
2. Guide to Listening Comprehension
3. Listening Guide
4. Listening Comprehension

Appendix

1 Basic Grammar

要增強英文閱讀理解能力，應練習找出英文的主結構。
要擁有良好的英語閱讀能力，首先要理解英文的段落結構。

「英文的主要句型結構比較簡單」

所有的英語文章都是由主詞和動詞所構成的，無論文章再怎麼長或複雜，它的架構一定是「主詞和動詞」，而「補語」和「受詞」是做補充主詞和動詞的角色。

某樣東西（人、事、物）　如何做

He runs (very fast). It is raining.

他 跑 （非常快） 雨 正在下

主詞　動詞　補語　補充的話

某樣東西（人、事、物）　如何做　怎麼樣

This is a cat. The cat is very big.

這 是 一隻貓。 那隻貓 是 非常 大

主詞 — 動詞 — 受詞

某樣東西　如何做　什麼
人、事、物

人，事物，
兩者皆是受詞

I like you. You gave me some flowers.

我 喜歡 你。 你 給 我 一些花

主詞 — 動詞 — 受詞 — 補語

某樣東西　如何做　什麼　怎麼樣／什麼
人、事、物

You make me happy. I saw him running.

你 使（讓）我 幸福（快樂） 我 看到 他 跑

其他修飾語或副詞等，都可以視為為了完成句子而臨時、額外、特別附加的，閱讀起來便可更加輕鬆；先具備這些基本概念，再閱讀本書的部分精選篇章，最後做了解文章整體架構的練習。

One day, the rich merchant suddenly lost everything.
有一天　富有的商人　突然　失去　一切

All of his ships sank.
他所有的船　沈沒

Now he only had a small country-house.
現在　他　只　有　一間鄉村小屋

The old merchant told his daughters what happened.
老商人　告訴　她的女兒們　發生了什麼事

Beauty said to her father, "Please don't cry.
美麗 說 對 他父親 「請不要哭」

We have each other and our good health.
我們 有 彼此 和 我們的健康

Money is not important."
錢 不是 重要的

Her sisters started to pull their hair out.
她的姐姐們 開始 拉扯 她們的頭髮

"Oh, father," the eldest daughter cried. "What will we do now?"
喔，父親 最大的女兒 喊叫 現在我們該怎麼辦

"You 'll have to work," he said, very sadly.
妳 必須工作 他說 很傷心地

The middle daughter was angry and said,
二女兒 是 生氣 並 說

"We can't work. No rich man will want to marry us!"
我們 不能工作 沒有有錢人 會想 娶 我們

One day, her father came home with a big smile.
有一天 她父親 回來 家裡 帶著大大的微笑

"I just heard some good news," he said.
我 剛才 聽到 好消息 他說

"One of my ships didn't sink.
我的其中一艘船 沒有沈

It 's bringing back lots of gold for us.
它 帶 回 很多黃金 為我們

We 'll be rich again!"
我們 將會 富有 再度

Beauty smiled at her father.
美麗 微笑 對她父親

"That 's great news.
那 是 好消息

I 'm so glad to see you happy again."
我 是 如此 高興 看你再開心起來

The two elder sisters jumped up for joy.
兩個姐姐 跳起來 因為喜悅

"We 're rich! We 're rich!" they shouted.
我們 是 富有的 我們 是 富有的 她們 喊叫

The next morning, Beauty's father woke up early.
第二天早上 美麗的父親 起床 很早

He had to meet his ship at the port.
他 要去會合 他的船 在港口

"Good-bye, girls. I 'm going to the port now," he said.
再見 女孩們 我 將去 港口 現在 他說

The elder sisters jumped out of bed and ran to their father.
姐姐們 跳 從床上 並 跑 到她們父親

"We had to eat bad food and wear ugly clothes," they said.
我們 得吃 糟糕的食物 和 穿 難看的衣服 她們說

"Will you bring us a present?"
會 你 帶來 我們 禮物

Appendix 2

Guide to Listening Comprehension

Use your book's CD to enjoy the audio version. When listening to the story, use some of the techniques shown below. If you take time to study some phonetic characteristics of English, listening will be easier.

Get in the flow of English.

English creates a rhythm formed by combinations of strong and weak stress intonations. Each word has its particular stress that combines with other words to form the overall pattern of stress or rhythm in a particular sentence.

When you are speaking and listening to English, it is essential to get in the flow of the rhythm of English. It takes a lot of practice to get used to such a rhythm. So, you need to start by identifying the stressed syllable in a word.

Listen for the strongly stressed words and phrases.

In English, key words and phrases that are essential to the meaning of a sentence are stressed louder. Therefore, pay attention to the words stressed with a higher pitch. When listening to an English recording for the first time, what matters most is to listen for a general understanding of what you hear. Do not try to hear every single word. Most of the unstressed words are articles or auxiliary verbs, which don't play an important role in the general context. At this level, you can ignore them.

Pay attention to liaisons.

In reading English, words are written with a space between them. There isn't such an obvious guide when it comes to listening to English. In oral English, there are many cases when the sounds of words are linked with adjacent words.

For instance, let's think about the phrase "**take off**," which can be used in "take off your clothes." "Take off your clothes" doesn't sound like [teɪk ɔ:f] with each of the words completely and clearly separated from the others. Instead, it sounds as if almost all the words in context are slurred together, [ˋteɪkɔ:f], for a more natural sound.

Shadow the voice of the native speaker.

Finally, you need to mimic the voice of the native speaker. Once you are sure you know how to pronounce all the words in a sentence, try to repeat them like an echo. Listen to the book again, but this time you should try a fun exercise while listening to the English.

This exercise is called "shadowing." The word "shadow" means a dark shade that is formed on a surface. When used as a verb, the word refers to the action of following someone or something like a shadow. In this exercise, pretend you are a parrot and try to shadow the voice of the native speaker.

Try to mimic the reader's voice by speaking at the same speed, with the same strong and weak stresses on words, and pausing or stopping at the same points.

Experts have already proven this technique to be effective. If you practice this shadowing exercise, your English speaking and listening skills will improve by leaps and bounds. While shadowing the native speaker, don't forget to pay attention to the meaning of each phrase and sentence.

Listen to what you want to shadow many times. Start out by just trying to shadow a few words or a sentence.

Mimic the CD out loud. You can shadow everything the speaker says as if you are singing a round, or you also can speak simultaneously with the recorded voice of the native speaker.

As you practice more, try to shadow more. For instance, shadow a whole sentence or paragraph instead of just a few words.

Appendix

3 Listening Guide

以下為《美女與野獸》各章節的前半部。一開始若能聽清楚發音，之後就沒有聽力的負擔。先聽過摘錄的章節，之後再反覆聆聽括弧內單字的發音，並仔細閱讀各種發音的說明。以下都是以英語的典型發音為基礎，所做的簡易說明，即使這裡未提到的發音，也可以配合音檔反覆聆聽，如此一來聽力必能更上層樓。

30 Chapter One page 14

Once, there was a rich (❶) in a big town. He had many ships. They brought (❷) (   ) gold from all over the world. He also had three (❸).

❶ **merchant** [ˋmɝtʃənt]：第一音節為重音，重音的下一個音節聽起來會相對較弱。

❷ **lots of** [lɑts əf]：lots 的 -s 和 of 連在一起，聽起來就像一個單字，尤其當 of 前面的單字字尾是子音時，唸出來十之八九是連音，而 of 所發的 [v] 音，通常聽不太出來。

❸ **daughters** [ˋdɔtɚz]：第一音節為重音，[ɔ] 與 [ə] 母音之間的 t，發出來會變成 [d] 的音，這是美式英語常見的發音。

31

Chapter Two page 28

When the old man walked home, the weather (❶) terribly cold. (❷) ( ) man (❸) ( ) and very cold. He thought it would be so miserable to sleep in the cold.

❶ **became** [bɪˋkem]：重音在第二音節，所以字首 be- 的發音聽起來微弱，不注意聽的話甚至會把單字誤聽為 came。

❷ **The old** [ði old]：old 的第一音節為母音，因此前面的 the 發音為 [i]，此處 old 最後的 [d] 音幾乎聽不到。

❸ **was sad** [wɑz sæd]：was 的 s 和 sad 連在一起時，兩個 s 只發音一次，如果有兩個相同或相似的音連在一起時，通常只發一次音，因此 was sad 聽起來會只有一個 [s] 的音。

32

Chapter Three page 44

The (❶) ( ), Beauty left for the castle. he asked people for (❷) . The castle was very famous, because it was the (❸) one around. At sunset she reached it. Beauty (❹) ( ) the castle. Like her father, she saw nobody.

❶ **next morning** [nɛkst ˋmɔrnɪŋ]：next 和 morning 這兩個字連在一起時，[t] 的發音通常不會唸出來。

❷ **directions** [dəˋrɛkʃənz]：重音在第二音節，第一、第三音節的母音發音微弱，強調重點在 [e]。

❸ **biggest** [ˋbɪgəst]：重音在第一音節，後面的 st 輕快地帶過。

❹ **looked around** [lʊkt əˋraʊnd]：這兩個單字連在一起時，around 的 字首 [ə] 幾乎不發音。

33

Chapter Four page 58

A week later, the Beast returned to the dining room. He looked (❶) and sad. "Beauty," he said. "I know (❷) I'm a beast. And I know that a beauty (❸) never marry a beast. Please, I'll just ask one thing of you. I (❹) (   ) to stay with me here forever.

❶ **embarrassed** [ɪm`bærəst]：重音在第二音節的 bar，母音的發音法是把嘴往兩邊用力張開，發出 [æ] 的音。

❷ **that** [ðæt]：關係代名詞 that 在句中非重點字，通常輕輕帶過。

❸ **could** [kʊd]：助動詞 could 放在句中時，也都發得很輕。

❹ **want you** [wɑnt ju]：want 的最後一個字母 t 和 you [ju] 連在一起時，通常會把唸成連音，發成 [tʃ] 的音。

34

Chapter Five page 72

A few evenings later, Beauty had a terrible dream. In the dream, she walked around the castle and (❶) ( ) the Beast. There was nobody there. She called his name, but she (❷) hear an answer.

❶ **looked for** [lʊkt fɔr]：looked 和 for 連在一起時，ed [t] 的音可能會消失，因為連續三個子音在一起時，中間的音常會略過。

❷ **didn't**：didn't 的 [t]，發音微弱，因為文章裡的 didn't 發音原本就很弱。

Appendix 4

Listening Comprehension

35 **A** Circle the correct answer.

1. Beauty (turned / returned) to her home.
2. Beauty (wants / went to) the Beast's Castle.
3. The ships have arrived at the (port / fort).
4. May I have (supper / suffer) with you?
5. The old merchant (lost / roast) all of his money.
6. Beauty (found / find) the Beast dying.

36 **B** Listen to the CD and finish the sentences.

1. They don't live in the city anymore. Now they live in the ___________.
2. These clothes are not cheap. They are ___________.
3. He isn't greedy at all. In fact, he's quite ___________.
4. She is not a good witch at all. She's an ___________witch.
5. Beauty can't leave the castle. She must ___________.

37 **C** Write down what you heard and circle either True or False.

T F ❶ ______________________________

T F ❷ ______________________________

T F ❸ ______________________________

38 **D** Listen to the CD and write down the question.

❶ ______________________________?

(a) Nice clothes.

(b) Good food.

(c) A rose.

❷ ______________________________?

(a) It sunk.

(b) It was robbed by pirates.

(c) It burned down.

❸ ______________________________?

(a) Because he took a rose.

(b) Because he didn't paid for his food.

(c) Because he slept late.

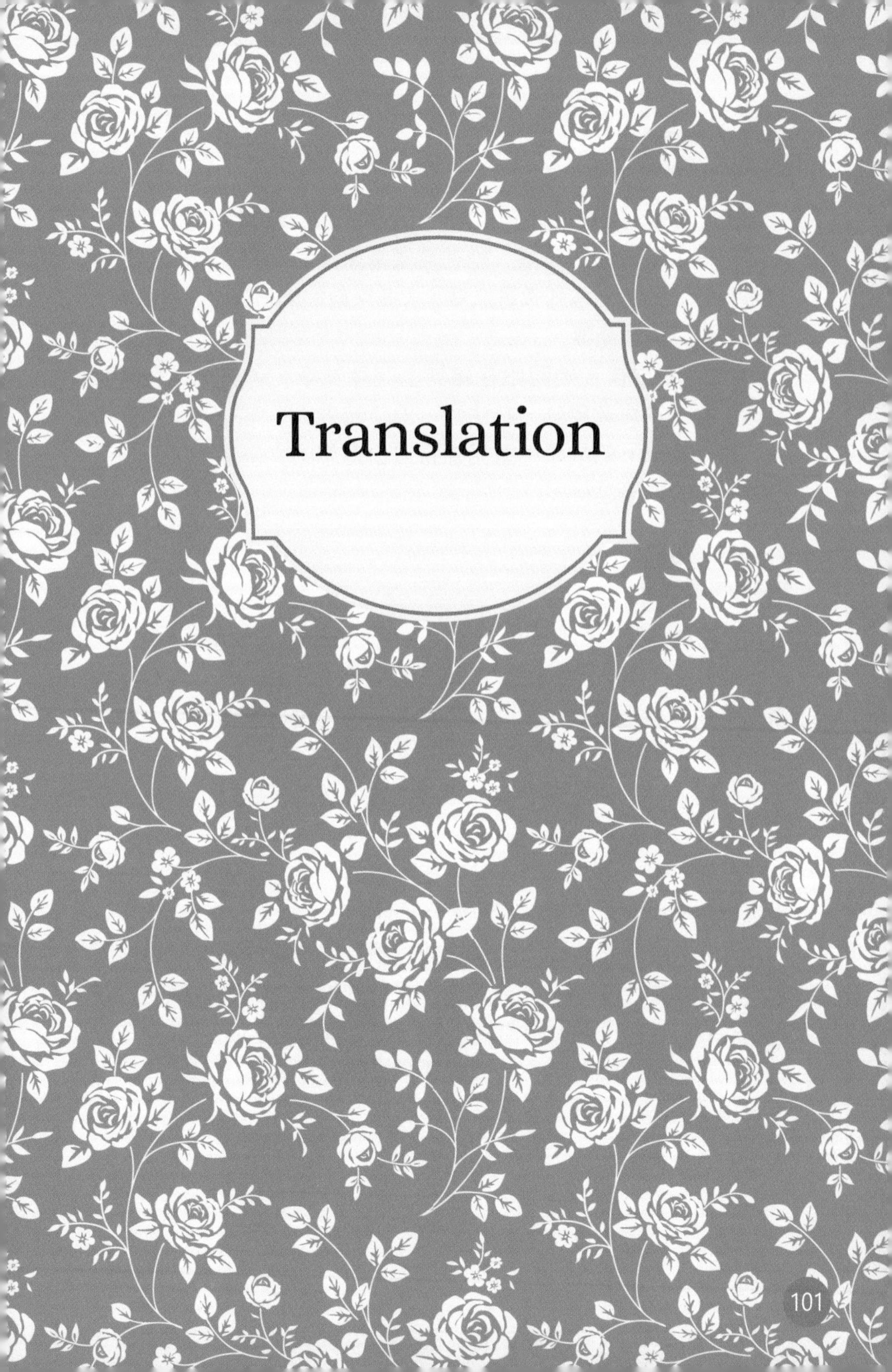

Translation

作者簡介

波茫特夫人（Beaumont, Madame de, 1711–1780）是位法國作家，婚後遷居英國。她在英國當家庭教師時，也開始在倫敦的報紙上撰寫一系列教育文章，大多來自民間傳說、歷史故事、傳奇故事與地理知識。

年屆 40 歲後，她開始在雜誌上刊登文章，《美女與野獸》便是登於一本兒童雜誌。在法國，波茫特夫人是第一個創辦兒童雜誌者。她筆下的故事與童話揉合自由幻想的文學潮流，乃浪漫主義文學的先驅之一。

故事介紹

《美女與野獸》是一位美麗少女與一隻野獸的故事。

很久很久以前，一位富商有三個女兒。三人之中，小女兒最漂亮善良。有一天，載滿商人所有家產的船隻皆遭遇船難，商人因此喪盡家產。商人聽聞其中一艘本以為失蹤已久的船，載著他的家產已入港，便滿懷希望地出發前往。然而，他到了港口才發現，連最後一艘船也被海盜占領了。

回家途中，可憐的商人借宿在野獸的城堡裡，因為摘了一朵玫瑰想作為小女兒的禮物，而激怒了野獸。

商人保證會將美麗的小女兒送給野獸，才終於毫髮無傷地回到家。為了信守承諾，美麗的小女兒前往城堡。因為野獸的內在美與好心腸，她不顧野獸醜陋的外貌，漸漸愛上了他。

《美女與野獸》是不分老少都喜愛的童話故事。這個故事也被製作成了迪士尼的動畫電影。

第一章　帶一朵玫瑰給我

p. 14–15 很久以前，在一個大城市裡有個富有的商人。他擁有許多艘商船，從世界各地買回大量的黃金。

商人有三位女兒，年長的兩個女兒，認為自己艷冠群芳，只穿最昂貴的服飾，只想著嫁入豪門。但小女兒則不會然。她是三個女兒中最美麗的，事實上，她所有的一切都是美好的，這也是她被取名為「美麗」的原因。

p. 16–17 有一天，這名商人一夕之間破產：他的商船全數沉沒，如今只剩下一間小小的鄉間住宅。

老商人把事情告訴女兒時，美麗對父親說：「請不要哭，我們還有彼此，還有健康的身體。錢並不是最重要的。」

她的兩個姐姐則開始扯著頭髮大叫。「喔，父親，現在我們該怎麼辦才好？」大女兒叫道。

「你們得去工作了。」他哀傷不已地說。

二女兒很生氣地答道：「我們不能去工作，那樣就沒有有錢人會娶我們了！」

p. 18–19 大女兒說：「我們到城裡去。嫁給第一個向我們求婚的人。」兩個姐姐便穿上最華麗的衣服，往城裡出發去找丈夫了，但人盡皆知商人所遭遇的變故了。

二姐對一個男人說：「我準備好結婚了。」男人回答：「我當初想娶妳，不過是為了妳的錢！」

另一個男人則對大姐說：「妳現在沒錢，所以我改變主意了。」然而，卻有一個男人來找美麗，對她說：「請嫁給我吧！我們可以快樂地生活在一起。」但她不能離開父親，她說：「我父親老了，我得陪他。」

p. 20–21 他們一家人搬到了鄉間小屋。兩個姐姐滿口抱怨，什麼事也不做。
美麗則每天辛勤地工作著，她想：「我要是不工作，父親就會挨餓的。」

一天，父親帶著一臉笑容回家。「我剛聽到一個好消息！」他說：「我有一艘船沒有沈，它正滿載著黃金回來了，我們又得回財富了！」

美麗對父親微笑道：「真是個好消息，真高興看到您又快樂起來了。」

兩個姐姐則是開心地跳了起來，直喊著：「我們有錢了！我們有錢了！」

p. 22–23 第二天，美麗的父親一早就起床，他得去港口接船。

「女兒們，再見！我要去港口了。」他說。

兩個姐姐立刻從床上跳起，跑向父親，説道:「我們粗茶淡飯、一身爛衣服的。」

「你會幫我們帶禮物回來嗎？我們要巧克力和幾件絲質洋裝。」

「沒問題，你們要的我會帶回來。」他說：「那妳呢，美麗？要我帶什麼給妳？」

看到父親開心，她就心滿意足，只想到了個簡單的東西。「就帶一朵玫瑰花給我吧。」她説道。

p. 25 於是，商人向她們道過再見便出發了。老商人步行到港口，花了一個多星期才抵達。當他到達港口時，卻聽到一件可怕的消息。

他僅剩的這一艘船上並沒有財富，船遇到了海盜，被洗劫一空了。

美麗的父親跪倒在地上，開始痛哭了起來。他想：「我一定是被詛咒了。」他傷心地準備走回家。

第二章　為什麼偷我的玫瑰？

p. 28–29 在老商人回家的途中，天氣驟寒。老人傷心之餘，又覺得冰冷。他想，這麼冷，睡在外面太悽慘了。

傍晚時分，商人看到了一座城堡。「說不定城堡裡住著一位善良的王子，會讓我今晚借住一宿。」他喃喃道。

他走到城堡的大門前，喊道：「哈囉！」但沒人應門。

他從窗口往裡面望去，只見壁爐生著火，爐邊有張桌子，桌上擺著烤雞、馬鈴薯、蛋糕和熱咖啡。那些食物看起來是那麼美味，城堡裡看起來又是那麼溫暖。

於是他走進城堡，坐了下來，把食物一啖而盡。吃過晚餐後，他躺在一張舒服的床上，沉入夢鄉。

p. 30–31 清晨，老人醒過來，精神愉快。看見桌上擺滿了豐盛的早餐，老商人對城堡的主人充滿感激。他不知道城主是誰，但城主在寒冷與飢餓的夜晚中拯救了他。

老人決定要去向主人道謝，他在屋裡四處走動，只見精美的家具和一間間的大房間，卻空無一人。他便對著空蕩蕩的城堡道謝，喊道：「不管您是誰，謝謝您！」

p. 32–33 正要離開的時候，老人瞧見了一座花園，花園裡長著幾叢玫瑰。他想起了美麗要的東西。

就在老人伸手摘下玫瑰時，傳來了一聲響亮的咆哮聲。商人跳了起來，只見一頭野獸向他衝過來。

「你這下流的人！小偷！」野獸咆哮著：「我給你食物吃，給你床睡，結果你做了什麼？偷我的玫瑰！現在你得付出代價，我要殺了你！」

碎！碎！老人的心臟急遽跳動。「大人，求求您！請原諒我。我無意冒犯您，我只是想帶一朵玫瑰給我的小女兒。」

「這我不管！還有，不要叫我『大人』，我叫做野獸，我就是野獸。」

p. 34–35 接著，野獸思索了起來。「你說你有個女兒是吧？你可以走了，但是你得把你的女兒送來給我。你的女兒要是不來的話，我就殺了你和你一家人！」

老人知道野獸不是說著玩的，但是他並不打算把女兒送來。

老人說道：「野獸，我有困難，我沒錢送她過來呀。還有，家裡只有她在工作，要是她不在，我一家人就要挨餓了。」

「這你不用擔心。」野獸說：「從我的城堡裡拿些黃金，我有很多，那些黃金就給你的家人。」

p. 36–37 老人拿了一袋黃金，便走回家。當他抵達家門時，又疲憊又傷心。

兩個姐姐看到他的臉後，嘆了口氣，她們知道一定出了什麼事。

「我猜猜看，最後一艘船也沉了，我們還是一樣窮。」大女兒說道。

「錢的問題不用擔心，我們有很多。」商人說，他打開袋子，黃金散落了一地。兩個姐姐急忙將黃金塞滿口袋。

美麗看著父親，說：「我很擔心您，您看起來很傷心。」

「我的確是很傷心，因為這個禮物。」商人說著，拿出玫瑰，將它交給美麗，然後把野獸、城堡和玫瑰的事，說給女兒們聽。

p. 38–39 兩個姐姐對這些事根本毫不在乎，只顧著開心地把玩黃金，但美麗禁不住哭了起來：「喔，太可怕了，這都是我的錯。」

一會兒後，美麗冷靜地說，「我會去找野獸的，爸爸。」

美麗的父親看著她。

她說：「我們別無選擇。我不去，野獸就會殺了您和我們全家。」她一副心意已決的樣子。要勸阻她是沒有用的，美麗一向是說了就會去做。

第三章　野獸要吃了我！

p. 44–45 第二天早上，美麗出發前往城堡。她向人問路，那座城堡是很有名的，那是附近最大的一座城堡。向晚時，她抵達城堡了。

美麗看了看城堡四周，但她和父親一樣，什麼人也沒看到。她大喊：「哈囉！」但沒有回應。她走進城堡，看到滿桌的食物，美麗心忖：「這個野獸，一定是想把我養胖，我想他是要吃了我。」美麗吃光了桌上的食物。

吃完晚餐後，她在城堡裡四處走動，那裡有精美的窗簾和昂貴的地毯，但一個人也沒有。接著，她看到一間圖書室，裡面擺著上千本的書，但裡頭也沒有人在閱讀。過了一會兒，她走到一扇門前，上面有個牌子，寫著「美麗的房間」。

p. 46–47 「這是我的房間？說不定他不會殺了我，但他怎麼會知道我的名字呢？」她想。

美麗打開房門走進去，對她的房間感到驚異不已。房間裡布置著精緻家具，這個房間就和她的人一樣美麗。置身其中，令她備感愉快。

她微笑著跳上床，床上擺著一本書，書名寫著「美麗的書」。她把書打開，讀著第一頁，上面寫著：「美麗，歡迎妳。妳什麼都不用擔心，在這座城堡裡，沒有人會傷害妳。妳是這裡的公主，如果妳有任何需要，只管開口，看不見的人會為妳服務。」

p. 48–49 「我想見我可憐的父親，他現在一定非常傷心。」當美麗一說出這句話，她家的景象立刻出現在她面前的鏡子裡。

她看到父親坐在他最喜歡的椅子上，看起來很悲傷。她還看到兩個姐姐正把玩著黃金。

她想著：「他很快就會習慣沒有我的生活了，他會再快樂起來的。」

不一會兒後，她邊想著家人，就邊沉入夢鄉了。

p. 50–51 第二天，美麗獨自過了一整天。到了晚上，她坐下來準備享用一頓豐盛的晚餐。就在她拿起刀叉時，她聽到身後傳來一聲溫和的嗥叫。

「美麗，我可以和妳一起吃晚餐嗎？」野獸說。

「這是你的城堡，你可以隨心所欲做你想做的事。」美麗答道。

野獸回答道：「不，妳是這座城堡的公主，應該由妳來決定，我不想讓妳覺得不自在。」

「你好像很和善呢。」她說。

野獸抬起他粗亂的眉毛，沒想到她會這麼說。

「你說話很溫柔，」美麗繼續說道：「你的內在想必更勝於外在。」

野獸害羞地答道：「這我可不知道呢。謝謝妳這麼說，我來和妳一起吃晚餐好了。」

p. 52–53 那一晚，美麗和野獸坐著一起用晚餐。他們聊了很久，最後結束時，美麗發現野獸並不如想像地恐怖。

每天晚上，野獸都和她一起共用晚餐。他們會聊很多事，但野獸每晚都會問她一個問題：「我到底有多醜？」

而美麗總是會回答：「你的心是美麗的。」她的確認為如此。

「我或許很善良，但我怎麼說都是一頭野獸。」他說。

有一件奇怪的事情開始發生，美麗竟開始覺得野獸一點也不醜。在她眼裡，野獸變得很英俊。

野獸知道美麗不會說謊，雖他不信自己長得好看，但他也相信美麗看見了他內在的善良。

p. 54–55 野獸對美麗一見鍾情，但美麗是不可能會愛他。他想：「要去愛一頭醜陋的野獸，這太難了吧。」

他時常幻想他們已經結了婚，去想像這個並不困難，因為他們同住在一個屋簷下，吃相同的食物，每天晚上都聊上好幾個小時，就像一般的夫妻一樣。唯一不同的是：美麗並不愛他。

後來有一天，他再也按捺不住自己的感情。「我愛妳，美麗。」他說：「請嫁給我吧。」

美麗坐下來，看著野獸，注視良久。「但你是野獸，我無法想像嫁給一頭野獸，我很抱歉。」

野獸咆哮了一聲，便跑走了。那晚過後，野獸在房間待了一個星期沒出來，美麗得獨自用餐。

第四章　不要離開我

p. 58–59 一星期後，野獸回到飯廳，他看起來既尷尬又傷心。他說：「美麗，我知道我是一頭野獸，我也知道一位美女絕不會嫁給一頭野獸，我只想求妳一件事，我希望妳能永遠待在這裡陪著我，我們做朋友吧！如果妳離開了，我會很寂寞的，我想我會傷心地死去。」

美麗看著地上，紅著臉道：「很抱歉，野獸。我得回去陪我父親，昨天我從魔鏡中看到，他現在一個人住，我姐姐們都還是嫁人離開他了，他需要人照顧。」

p. 60–61 「我明白，美麗，妳是那麼善良。」野獸說：「我知道妳必須陪妳父親，但是我無法忍受孤獨，妳可以回家一個星期，我會送一些錢到妳家裡，請一位好的僕人照顧妳父親。妳之後再回來陪我，如果妳不回來，我會心碎而死。」

「好，野獸。」美麗說道，「我父親只要再見到我，就會很開心了。」

野獸說：「拿著這個戒指，戴上它吧。等妳要回來時，就在上床睡覺前把戒指摘下來，第二天早上，妳就會在我的城堡裡醒來。」

p. 62–63 美麗便戴著戒指上床睡覺。第二天清晨，她在父親的屋子裡醒過來。她看到房間的角落有一個箱子，裡面裝滿黃金，和綴著珠寶和由銀線所縫製的華服。

美麗知道這些是野獸送的禮物。「謝謝你，野獸。」她對自己說。

當孤獨的老商人一看到美麗，便哭了起來。他流下的，是歡喜的眼淚。

他說：「妳回來，是上天所賜的禮物，我還以為野獸把妳吃掉了。」

商人抱住女兒許久，兩人歡喜不已。

p. 64–65 幾天後，兩個姐姐帶著丈夫一起回來。她們各自嫁給了又富有又英俊的男子，可是這兩名丈夫卻讓姐姐們看起來不怎麼快樂。

美麗見到這兩名男人後，開始想到許多和野獸有關的事。這兩個人長相英俊，而野獸很醜；他們很乏味，但野獸很有趣；他們心地不好，野獸心地很善良；他們很吝嗇，野獸卻很大方；他們讓自己的妻子傷心，但野獸卻讓她很快樂。

美麗想著野獸，忍不住笑了。

一時之間，美麗明白自己愛上野獸了。二姐見到她在笑，不禁一股氣上來:「她看起來那麼快活，我卻這麼難過。這無法忍受，真希望她死掉！」

p. 66–67 「我有個辦法。」二姐對大姐說：「我們讓美麗無法如期回到城堡，那野獸就會很生氣，等她回去之後，野獸就會把她給吃了。」

大姐很贊同，她向來就很嫉妒美麗比她貌美。

「我們就對她好一點，那樣她就會不想離開了。」大姐說。

幾天過去了，兩個姐姐十分善待美麗。她們送她禮物，整理父親的房子，對美麗滿口好話。

「可憐的美麗，妳工作地這麼辛苦，」大姐說：「休息一下吧。」

p. 68–69 到了第六天，美麗到城裡去，找了一個好僕人，僕人當晚就和美麗一起回家。「父親，我給您找了一位僕人，她會好好照顧您的。現在，我得跟你們大家說再見了。」

大姐於是哭了起來。二姐說：「喔，妳不能離開我們呀，我們才要開始瞭解妳，我還想要多和妳說說話。」

大姐說：「拜託妳！拜託妳！再多待一個星期吧！」美麗不忍見她們傷心，便說：「好吧！那我就多留一個星期吧。」

第五章　野獸，我愛你！

p. 72–73 幾天過後，美麗做了一個惡夢。夢裡，她在城堡四周到處尋找野獸，卻見不到任何的身影；她叫著野獸的名字，卻聽不到任何的回應聲。

這時她聽到城堡附近有聲響，走過去一看，正是野獸，他正躺在地上。「喔，野獸，請不要死。」她哭喊道。

「我太醜了，對不對？」他叫道：「妳永遠不會喜歡像我這樣的野獸。」野獸說完，便在她懷中斷氣了。

美麗驚醒後跳下床。「我在做什麼？我會害死可憐的野獸的，我要立刻回去找野獸，嫁給他！」

美麗寫了一封信留給父親，然後拔下戒指，再次進入夢鄉。

p. 74–75 早上，美麗在城堡裡醒了過來。她到處尋找野獸，但沒找到。她想，晚餐時，野獸就會一如往常一樣地出現了吧。

「今晚，我會告訴他，我要嫁給他。」那天晚上，美麗將自己打扮得很漂亮。

然而晚餐時，她卻沒有看到任何食物如魔法般地出現，也沒有看到野獸。美麗心想：「他是不是死了？他會不會因為我沒有及時回來找他，所以死了？是不是我不願意嫁給他，所以他活不下去了？」

p. 76–77 「野獸！野獸！」她呼喊著，但沒有任何回應。她想起在夢中發現野獸的地方，便飛奔過去。她看到野獸正躺在花園裡，看起來就像快死了一樣，一如夢中所見。

「野獸，你不能死！」她哭喊道：「你要和我一起生活，做我的丈夫！拜託你，和我結婚吧！」

接著美麗將他瀕死的身軀轉過來，抱在懷中，親吻了野獸毛茸茸的臉頰。就在這時，她看到一道光閃過。

p. 78–79 忽然間，美麗發現自己身在城堡裡，房間裡擺滿了玫瑰，站在她身旁的是一位英俊的青年，穿著就像一位王子。她很困惑，「這是怎麼回事？我親愛的野獸在哪裡？」

「親愛的美麗，我就是妳的野獸。很久以前，邪惡的女巫對我施了咒語，把我變成一頭野獸。她說，除非有美麗的姑娘答應嫁給我，否則我就永遠不會變回原來的樣子，也不會老死。我獨自居住了幾百年，直到妳來到城堡，幾百年來，我第一次感到快樂。但當妳說不願意嫁給我，我覺得自己就快要死了。然後妳又回來說願意嫁給我，不但救了我一命，也讓我變回原本的樣子。妳有恩於我，親愛的美麗，而且我也非常愛妳。」

p. 80–81 就在此時，善良的女巫出現了。她對王子說：「殿下，很高興見到你恢復原來的樣子了。美麗，妳終於遇到一個像妳一樣美好的人了，你們的確是世界上最美好的一對，我要讓你們今天就結婚，讓你們下半輩子都能過著幸福快樂的日子，我還會帶給你們幸福美麗的孩子。」

從那天起，美麗和她的王子一生幸福。他們晚上照樣會長聊，孩子誕生後，城堡的廳廊不時充滿了孩子們的笑聲。

用字表

a
about
after
ago
all
actually
alright
again
always
agree
amaze
alone
an
also
angry
am
answer
amazed
any
and
anymore
another
anywhere
appear
anybody
arm
anything
around
apartment
as
are
asleep
armchair
back
arrive
bag
ask
be
at
away
awful
beat
bad
beauty
bathroom
become
beast
before
beautiful
behind
because
big
bed
blank
begin
book
believe
bend
best
bore
bird
borrow
blue
blush
boat
boy
bookshelf
bright
born
but
bottle
bottom
box
by
breakfast
call
bring
brink
bush
can
buy
candle
cake
care
carpet
cast
castle
chapter
cheek
chest
century
chair
chandelier
change
chicken
child
chocolate
chronological
circle
clock
choice
coffee
cold
come
clothe
complain
computer
column
continue
comfortable
corner
complete
comprehension
country-house
confuse
couple
creature
crosswords
curse
curtain
daughter
cry
day
dead
dear
decide
delicious
desk
determine
did
difficult
dine
dinnertime
die
different
direction
dirty
dinner
dish
do
down
drawer
dream
door
dress
downstairs
early
eat

either
each
elder
eldest
eh
else
empty
end
entire
embarrass
even
evening
every
everyday
everyone
everything
evil
expect
eyebrow
face
fact
expensive
fall
famous
fantastic
fat
family
father
fault
favorite
feel
feeling
few
fill
finally
fine
fire
fish
find
five
flash
fireplace
first
flower
food
for
floor
forever
follow
fork
form
four
forgive
French
friend
from
funny
furniture
front
full
future
garden
gate
generous
gentle
gently
get
give
glad
gift
girl
go
gold
golden
good-bye
grateful
great
good-looking
grandmother
greedy
grow
growl
grill
grind
guess
hair
hairy
hall
handsome
happen
happily
happiness
hard
have
happy
he
health
hear
heart
heartbreak
hello
her
heaven
here
herself
hide
hire
his
him
hold
home
hot
hour
house
how
hundred
hungry
hug
hurt
imagine
important
husband
if
in
inside
interest
into
invisible
it
jealous
jewel
join
joy
jump
joke
just
keep
kill
kind
king
kiss
kitchen
kneel
knife
know
lamp
land
last
late
laugh
laughter
lazy
learn
lay
least
leave
library
life
let
letter
like
lie
long
light

look
live
lonely
loud
loudly
lord
lose
lot
love
luck
magical
magically
make
man
many
marry
match
may
me
mean
maybe
meet
merchant
mind
mirror
middle
miserable
miss
moment
money
more
my
myself
morning
move
must
name
natural
nearby
napkin
need
never
news
next
nice
night
no
nobody
noise
not
nothing
now
ocean
of
off
offend
often
oh
OK
old
on
one
once
oneself
open
only
or
order
other
our
out
over
owe
owner
page
paint
paper
part
pencil
pay
people
person
pick
piano
picture
pillow
pirate
place
plan
play
poor
please
pocket
port
pot
potato
present
pretty
prince
princess
probably
problem
propose
put
pull
quickly
quietly
quiz
reach
rain
raise
ready
read
realize
rearrange
really
remember
refrigerator
relate
request
return
rest
ring
rewrite
rich
right
rise
roast
roof
rob
room
rose
sad
run
sadly
sadness
same
save
scary
say
sea
school
scientist
sea-princesses
second
see
seem
send
sentence
set
servant
shall
shampoo
she
ship
shout
shyly
sick
sigh
sign
silk
simple
silver
sink

sir
sister
sit
six
sixth
sky
sleep
small
smile
snow
so
soap
sofa
some
someone
something
soon
sorry
speak
spell
spend
spoon
stair
stand
star
start
starve
station
stay
steal
still
stingy
stool
stop
story
strange
suddenly
sun
sunrise
sunset
supper
sweet
swim
table
take
talk
tear
television
tell
tense
tennis
terrible
terribly
thank
than
that
the
then
their
them
there
these
they
thief
thing
think
thousand
this
three
through
time
thump
tire
title
to
today
together
toilet
tomorrow
tonight
too
toothbrush
toothpaste
towel
toward
town
travel
truly
try
TV
two
ugly
uncomfortable
under
underline
understand
uniform
until
up
upstairs
us
use
usual
vase
very
wake
walk
wall
want
wardrobe
warm
washstand
water
way
we
wear
weather
week
welcome
what
when
where
which
while
who
whoever
whole
why
wife
will
window
wise
wish
witch
with
without
woman
wonderful
word
work
world
worried
worry
would
write
wrong
year
yell
yesterday
you
young
your

Answers

P. 26	A	beautiful, nice, rose
	B	❶ T ❷ F ❸ T ❹ F
P. 27	C	❶ will bring ❷ will start ❸ will
	D	❹ → ❷ → ❸ → ❺ → ❶
P. 40	A	❶ saw ❷ ate ❸ looked ❹ walked
P. 41	B	❶ T ❷ F ❸ T
	C	❶ c ❷ d ❸ b ❹ a
	D	❸ → ❶ → ❷ → ❹
P. 56	A	painting, table, curtain, sign
	B	❶ appeared ❷ imagined ❸ spent ❹ believed
P. 57	C	❶ d ❷ a ❸ b ❹ c
	D	❹ → ❶ → ❷ → ❸
P. 70	A	❶ ugly ❷ interesting ❸ kind ❹ generous ❺ happy
	B	❶ T ❷ T ❸ F ❹ F ❺ F
P. 71	C	❶ left ❷ smile ❸ servant
	D	❶ d ❷ a ❸ c ❹ e ❺ b

P. 82	A	❶ wrote	❷ happy	❸ crying	❹ dressed
	B	❶ F	❷ T	❸ F	❹ T
P. 83	C	❶ didn't see any	❷ didn't cast	❸ were not	
	D	❹ → ❸ → ❺ → ❷ → ❶			

P. 98	A	❶ returned ❹ supper	❷ went to ❺ lost	❸ port ❻ found
	B	❶ country ❹ evil	❷ expensive ❺ stay	❸ generous

P. 99

C
❶ The Beast was always ugly. (F)
❷ The merchant was always poor. (F)
❸ Beauty was better-looking than her sisters. (T)

D
❶ What gift does Beauty ask for? (c)
❷ What happened to the Merchant's last ship? (b)
❸ Why was the Beast angry with the merchant? (a)

Adaptor of *"Beauty and the Beast!"*

David Desmond O'Flaherty

University of Carleton (Honors English Literature and Language)
Kwah-Chun Foreign Language High School, English Conversation Teacher

美女與野獸【二版】
Beauty and the Beast

作者 _ 波茫特夫人
（Beaumont, Madame de）
改寫 _ David Desmond O'Flaherty
插圖 _ Valentina Andreeva
翻譯 / 編輯 _ 羅竹君
作者 / 故事簡介翻譯 _ 王采翎
校對 _ 王采翎
封面設計 _ 林書玉
排版 _ 葳豐／林書玉
播音員 _ Fiona Steward, Michael Yancey
製程管理 _ 洪巧玲
發行人 _ 周均亮
出版者 _ 寂天文化事業股份有限公司
電話 _ +886-2-2365-9739
傳真 _ +886-2-2365-9835
網址 _ www.icosmos.com.tw
讀者服務 _ onlineservice@icosmos.com.tw
出版日期 _ 2019年8月 二版一刷（250201）
郵撥帳號 _ 1998620-0 寂天文化事業股份有限公司

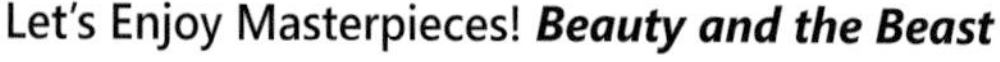

Let's Enjoy Masterpieces! *Beauty and the Beast*

國家圖書館出版品預行編目資料

美女與野獸【二版】 / Beaumont, Madame de 著 ; David Desmond O'Flaherty 改寫. —二版. —[臺北市] : 寂天文化, 2019.08 面 ; 公分. (Grade 1經典文學讀本)譯自 : Beauty and the Beast

ISBN 978-986-318-822-3 (25K平裝附光碟片)

1. 英語 2. 讀本

805.18 108012294